YASMIN

The Painter

written by
SAADIA FARUQI

illustrated by
HATEM ALY

PICTURE WINDOW BOOKS
a capstone imprint

To Mariam for inspiring me, and
Mubashir for helping me find the
right words —S.F.

To my sister, Eman, and her amazing
girls, Jana and Kenzi —H.A.

Yasmin is published by Picture Window Books,
a Capstone Imprint
1710 Roe Crest Drive
North Mankato, Minnesota 56003
www.mycapstone.com

Text © 2019 Saadia Faruqi
Illustrations © 2019 Picture Window Books

Cataloging-in-Publication Data is available on the Library of
Congress website.

ISBN: 978-1-5158-2728-3 (hardcover)
978-1-5158-2731-3 (paperback)
978-1-5158-2735-1 (ebook pdf)

Summary: Yasmin's painting for the art contest is due Friday, but
she has lots of excuses for putting it off. She doesn't know what
to paint, she doesn't think she's any good, and painting is messy.
Turns out a mess is just what Yasmin needs for inspiration!

Editor: Kristen Mohn
Designer: Aruna Rangarajan

Design Elements:
Shutterstock: Art and Fashion

Printed and bound in the United States of America.
PA021

TABLE OF CONTENTS

CHAPTER 1

The Announcement

On Monday in art class, Ms. Alex made an announcement.

"We're having an art competition on Friday night! I hope you all enter. The winner will get a special prize."

Everyone was really excited.

Everyone but Yasmin. Yasmin
was worried.

She wasn't very good at
art. Her circles were always
lopsided.

And her hearts
never looked like
hearts at all.

"What's the prize?"
Ali asked.

"That's a surprise,"
Ms. Alex replied.

Yasmin frowned.

On Tuesday evening Baba came home with a box. "Yasmin, I have a present for you!" he called.

Yasmin ran downstairs. What was it? A new puzzle? A craft kit?

Baba helped her open the box. "Oh," said Yasmin. "Paints."

"Yes, for the art competition on Friday. Look, there's an easel, and canvas too!" Baba said.

Yasmin wrinkled her nose. But she said, "Thank you, Baba," and took the supplies upstairs.

CHAPTER 2

Yasmin Makes a Mess

On Wednesday after school, Mama showed Yasmin videos of famous artists. There was a man with a bow tie who was painting trees. There was an old woman painting mountains.

Yasmin thought of her own messy, ugly artwork. She sighed. "I'll never be as good as they are."

Mama smiled. "It's OK, jaan. You only have to try your best."

But Yasmin still wasn't ready to paint.

On Thursday Mama said, "Yasmin, finish your schoolwork while I make dinner."

Yasmin watched the video of the man with the bow tie again. He made it look so easy. She decided to give it a try.

She set up the easel and paints and tried to copy him.

A tree was easy,

wasn't it? No.

Maybe a little

flower? No.

Her pictures looked

nothing like the ones on the

video. Yasmin stomped her

foot in frustration.

Oops! Everything scattered

around her. What a mess!

Then she noticed something.
Yellow paint had splashed on
the top part of her canvas. She
thought it looked like the sun.

She took some

brown paint and

splashed it on

the canvas too.

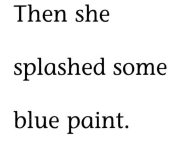

Then she

splashed some

blue paint.

Then some green

paint.

Soon Yasmin's

idea was taking shape.

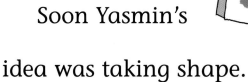

CHAPTER 3

Competition Day

On Friday night Mama and Baba walked with Yasmin to her school. It was weird—and exciting!—to go to school at night.

Ms. Alex had decorated the cafeteria with balloons.

"Welcome, children!" she said brightly. "I can't wait to see what you've created!"

Yasmin had a strange feeling in her tummy, like a hundred soda pop bubbles.

Principal Nguyen was the judge.

He looked at Ali's mountains and

Emma's basketball. He carefully

studied each student's work.

Yasmin pretended to drink her punch. Mama squeezed her shoulder. "Don't worry. Your painting is beautiful!"

Soon Mr. Nguyen tapped the microphone. "The winner of the competition is . . . Yasmin Ahmad!"

Yasmin couldn't believe it.

Her splotchy meadow painting

had won!

But wait—what was the

mystery prize?

A man entered the cafeteria. It was the painter from the videos!

"Yasmin, so nice to meet you!" he said. "For your prize I'll be giving you painting lessons next week."

"Thank you! But I have to warn you, I'll probably make a mess!" Yasmin replied.

The artist laughed. "Don't worry. I will too!"

Think About It, Talk About It

* Yasmin doesn't think she's a very good artist. Why does she feel that way? If Yasmin were your friend, what would you say to her?

* What special skill or talent do you have? What special talent do you wish you had? Can you think of ways you could practice to get better at your talents?

* Some accidents are bad, but some accidents are good! Yasmin's painting started from a happy accident. Have you ever had something go wrong that turned out to be something good?

Learn Urdu with Yasmin!

Yasmin's family speaks both English and Urdu. Urdu is a language from Pakistan. Maybe you already know some Urdu words!

baba (BAH-bah)—father

hijab (HEE-jahb)—scarf covering the hair

jaan (jahn)—life; a sweet nickname for a loved one

kameez (kuh-MEEZ)—long tunic or shirt

mama (MAH-mah)—mother

naan (nahn)—flatbread baked in the oven

nana (NAH-nah)—grandfather on mother's side

nani (NAH-nee)—grandmother on mother's side

salaam (sah-LAHM)—hello

sari (SAHR-ee)—dress worn by women in South Asia

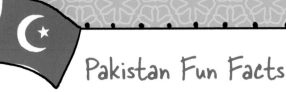

Pakistan Fun Facts

Yasmin and her family are proud of their Pakistani culture. Yasmin loves to share facts about Pakistan!

Location

Pakistan is on the continent of Asia, with India on one side and Afghanistan on the other.

Islamabad

PAKISTAN

Capital

Islamabad is the capital, but Karachi is the largest city.

Sports

Pakistan is the largest producer of handmade soccer balls in the world.

Nature

The longest river in Pakistan is the Indus River. A very rare type of dolphin lives there.

Make a Flower Motif Bookmark

SUPPLIES:

- white cardstock
- scissors
- ruler
- pencil
- colored pencils

STEPS:

1. Use ruler and pencil to measure a rectangle bookmark on your paper 2 inches (5 cm) wide and 6 inches (15 cm) long. Cut out the bookmark.

2. On a separate piece of paper, practice drawing the flower in simple steps, as shown.

3. Draw three or four of the flower designs on your bookmark, depending on the size of your drawing.

4. Have fun coloring your bookmark!

About the Author

Saadia Faruqi is a Pakistani American writer, interfaith activist, and cultural sensitivity trainer previously profiled in *O Magazine*. She is author of the adult short-story collection, *Brick Walls: Tales of Hope & Courage from Pakistan*. Her essays have been published in *Huffington Post*, *Upworthy*, and *NBC Asian America*. She resides in Houston, Texas, with her husband and children.

Hatem Aly is an Egyptian-born illustrator whose work has been featured in multiple publications worldwide. He currently lives in beautiful New Brunswick, Canada, with his wife, son, and more pets than people. When he is not dipping cookies in a cup of tea or staring at blank pieces of paper, he is usually drawing books. One of the books he illustrated is *The Inquisitor's Tale* by Adam Gidwitz, which won a Newbery Honor and other awards, despite Hatem's drawings of a farting dragon, a two-headed cat, and stinky cheese.

Join Yasmin on all her adventures!

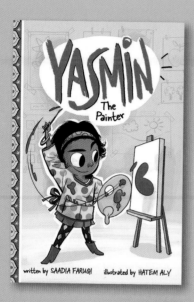

YASMIN
The Painter

written by SAADIA FARUQI   illustrated by HATEM ALY

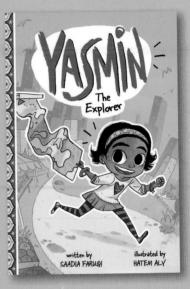

YASMIN
The Explorer

written by
SAADIA FARUQI   illustrated by
HATEM ALY

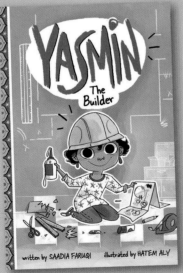

YASMIN
The Builder

written by SAADIA FARUQI   illustrated by HATEM ALY

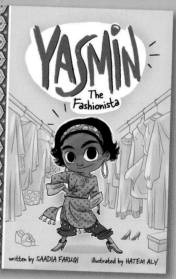

YASMIN
The Fashionista

written by SAADIA FARUQI   illustrated by HATEM ALY

Discover more at
www.capstonekids.com